NEWT

BIG CITY DREAMS

This book is dedicated to Rosalie, Melvin Morris, and Todd Marrone

Aces Klick Books
Copyright© 2014 by Nahjee Grant
Illustrated by Anthony Joshua
Coloring by Brian Oliver
Page Edits by Maurice Jackson Jr
"TweenerCity" ®, "NEWIE" ® are registered trademarks of Aces Klick WorldWide
LLC.

For more information visit:
www.tweenercity.com
www.acesklick.com

Newie decides to follow his dream to sing against his father's wishes. This decision will take Newie on a journey to a dangerous city full of trickery and broken dreams. If Newie continues to believe in himself all of his dreams will come true and there is no turning back for him now. Or is there? Let's begin Newie's adventure together and find out.

After jumping off the truck that brought them to the city, a wide eyed Newie and Wilbo look at each other and bravely start to walk into a frightening big city.

Newie and Wilbo dodge walking pedestrians as they escape from being squashed by their giant feet.

Newie angrily looks up and yells at the large people "hey watch where you're walking!"

The humans look down at Newie and Wilbo in amazement and shock, "Is that a fish?" the woman asks. "No it's a Newt and it talks!" her husband gasps.

"Awe Mommy he's so cute can I keep him?" the little girl asks. "I'll take good care of him I promise, I will name him Choochie".

The girl picks Newie up in
her hand with great force.

"You're all mine now little Choochie you will be my pet forever and ever" the girl screams with delight. She then squeezes Newie tight with two hands and smiles with an evil grin, "yikes Wilbo help!" Newie squeals.

Thinking quickly Wilbo stings the girl on her hand so New-ie can escape from her clutches.

The plan works and Newie falls and lands swiftly to the ground. "Whew that was a close one Wilbo!" said Newie, "thanks buddy let's get out of here."

They find a hole in the wall nearby. "Run Wilbo we have to get away from her" Newie says in a panicky hurry.

"That was scary Wilbo" Newie says as he catches his breath. "Maybe we don't belong in the city. I guess father was right about this place and what is a pet Wilbo?"

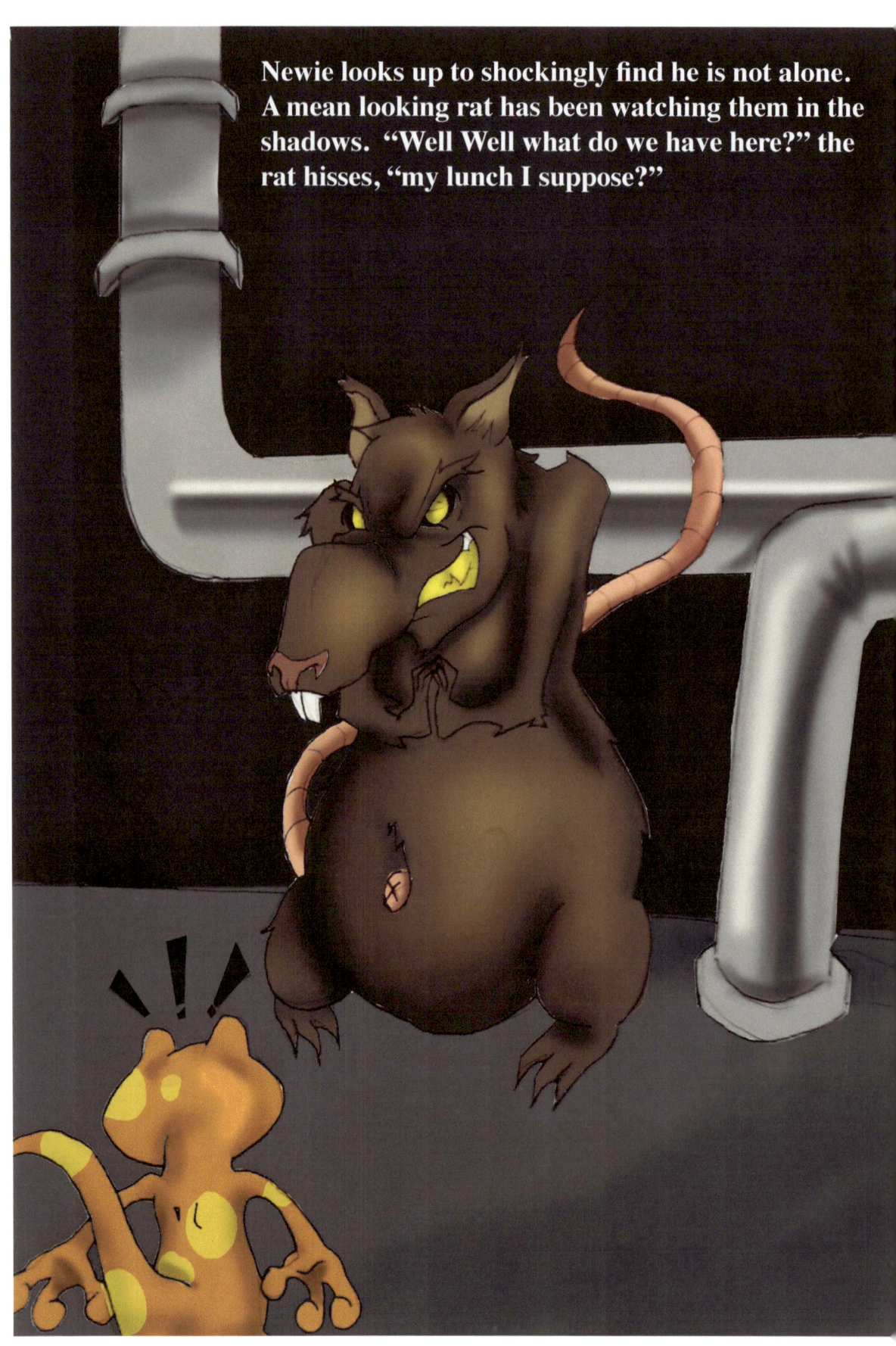

They try to run but are suddenly in the hands of the giant rat and quickly caught. "Oh no not again Wilbo he's going to eat us. Please don't eat us Mr. Rat" Newie whined.

"Hey", the rat replied, "my name is Tom and I'm not as spooky as I look. Plus I already ate my dinner, I'm not hungry" he laughed.

"Here is some advice if you want to survive in the city", says Tom, "you have to be confident and believe in yourself. Stick your chest out a little kid", he added, "let everybody know you're the boss and not afraid, especially those jokers in the pet shop."

Newie and Wilbo make their way into the next room, Tom waves good bye and wishes him good luck. "Thank you Tom, Newie replies, "I hope to see you again soon".

A confident Newie walks into the pet store with his head held high. "Newie do you want to go back home?" Wilbo asked, "I'm sure your father is worried."

Before Newie answers he is suddenly stopped by a strange sound. "Do you hear that Wilbo?" Newie pointed out, "It's amazing! Where is it coming from?"

Newie continues, "I think the sound is coming from up there Wilbo" as he points to the cage. They begin to climb up the counter all the way to the top.

After a long struggle to the top Newie is so surprised
he's stuck in a daze and Wilbo almost faints.

They see a group of friendly birds singing and dancing in their cage.

Newie is so thrilled he sits down and applauds the bird's performance. "Wow this is great Wilbo!" Newie giggled.

Newie raises his hand on his hip with confidence "just wait one minute my feathered friends, I'm a singer too" Newie bragged.

The angry birds huddle together "what do you want to do with the newt Sunny?" one bird asks.
"Are any of you hungry?" Sunny replied. Newie looks very confused "I wonder what they're talking about Wilbo?" Newie mumbled.

The hungry birds turn to Newie and Wilbo with a strange look "I think its dinner time boys!" Sunny huffs as he fits his bib around his neck with a hungry look in his eyes.

Newie is once again in shock and pleads for help "you're not going to eat us are you?!"

The birds begin to chase him across the cage as Newie dashes
out of danger and runs to keep from being eaten!

Newie is now corned in the cage trembling and shaking in fear.
"Maybe we should have gone home Wilbo this city is creepy"
Newie cries.

He decides to be fearless and confidently show the birds he has what it takes and sings to the top of his lungs!

All of the animals in the pet store hear Newie's wonderful voice. They are amazed by his talents, even the hungry birds.

While he is singing at the top of his lungs Newie is picked up by two very large hands. "Well what do we have here?" an unknown voice Newie hears.

A confused Newie opens one eye still afraid to open the other "Is that you Wilbo?" he whispers.

Newie's magnificent singing drew a crowd outside the pet store too. "Look honey is that newt singing?" the husband asks.

"He's awesome! Mommy can I have him?!" a little boy shouts in excitement, "He sounds cool".

The store owner places Newie on a table and leans over to him. "Hey little guy you sure can sing a great tune, how would you like to live here with me and sing full time?"

"Wow Wilbo I finally did it they love me! I bet father would be so proud of me!"

Will Newie's father approve of him sneaking to the city?

Will Newie ever meet Marco again and his band from the first book?

Will the store owner make Newie a singing star?

Stay tuned to find out and continue the journey!

Believe in Newie and most importantly BELIEVE IN YOURSELF!

BIG CITY DREAMS

www.ingramcontent.com/pod-product-compliance
Lightning Source LLC
Chambersburg PA
CBHW041000170626
46815CB00002B/96